Animal Fairy Tales

The Kitten Who Cried Dog

written by Charlotte Guillain ☆ illustrated by Dawn Beacon

Raintree

Chicago, Illinois

© 2013 Raintree
an imprint of Capstone Global Library, LLC
Chicago, Illinois

To contact Capstone Global Library please phone 800-747-4992, or visit our website
www.capstonepub.com

Edited by Daniel Nunn, Rebecca Rissman, and Sian Smith
Designed by Joanna Hinton-Malivoire
Original illustrations © Capstone Global Library, Ltd., 2013
Illustrated by Dawn Beacon
Production by Victoria Fitzgerald
Originated by Capstone Global Library, Ltd.
Printed in China

16 15 14 13 12
10 9 8 7 6 5 4 3 2 1

Library of Congress Cataloging-in-Publication Data
Guillain, Charlotte.
  The kitten who cried dog / Charlotte Guillain.
      p. cm. -- (Animal fairy tales)
Summary: A simplified version of the familiar fable featuring a kitten who becomes bored
with guarding a stack of toys and decides to cry "dog" and watch the villagers come
running, until the day a dog is really there and no one answers his call. Includes a note on
the history of the tale.
  ISBN 978-1-4109-5023-9 (hb) -- ISBN 978-1-4109-5029-1 (pb) -- ISBN 978-1-4109-5041-3
(big book) [1. Fables. 2. Folklore.] I. Aesop. II. Title.

PZ8.2.G85Kit 2013
398.2—dc23   2012017425
[E]

Characters

kitten

 the villagers

a little lamb

a fluffy bunny

a naughty dog

Once upon a time, there was a village full of cats. The villagers had a fine collection of toys, but they were worried about a naughty dog who lived nearby. The naughty dog wanted to steal their toys!

The villagers decided it would be one kitten's job to guard the toys. "Keep a close eye on the toys!" they told him.

"If the dog comes to steal them, cry out 'Dog!' as loudly as you can!"

At first, the kitten felt very important.

But after a while, he began to feel bored.
His job was not much fun.

The bored kitten decided to trick the
other villagers. When a little lamb ran
near the toys, the kitten cried out,

"Dog! Dog!"

All the villagers ran to the kitten
as quickly as they could. When they
reached him, they were very angry.

They told the kitten not to shout out
again unless the naughty dog really
did come near.

So, the kitten went back to guarding the toys. But after a while, he became bored again.

When a fluffy bunny hopped near
the toys, once again he shouted,

"Dog! Dog!"

Once again, the villagers all ran to help
the kitten. When they saw the dog was
not there, they were furious!

The villagers left the kitten to guard
the toys once more.

When the kitten was all alone, the naughty dog suddenly ran up to him!

The kitten was terrified! He shouted out,

"Dog! Dog!"

But this time nobody came. The naughty dog ran away with all of the toys.

The kitten went to find the villagers
and told them the dog had stolen the
toys. "We didn't come because you lied
to us before!" they meowed.

The kitten had to work hard for a very
long time before he could buy new toys
for all the villagers.

The end

Where does this story come from?

You've probably already heard the story that *The Kitten Who Cried Dog* is based on—*The Boy Who Cried Wolf*. There are many different versions of this story. When people tell a story, they often make little changes to make it their own. How would you change this story?

The history of the story

The Boy Who Cried Wolf story is supposed to have been told in Ancient Greece by a storyteller called Aesop. Aesop is thought to have written many fables (stories that have a moral at the end). The characters in fables always learn something from the way they have behaved.

In the original story, a shepherd boy keeps calling out to nearby villagers for help, telling them a wolf is attacking his sheep when nothing has actually happened. In the end they ignore him, so when a wolf really does turn up nobody comes to help him. The moral of the story is that if you keep telling lies, people will stop believing anything you say, even if you are telling the truth. Today, people use the expression "to cry wolf" when someone has raised a false alarm.